Please feel free to send me an email. Just know that these emails are filtered by my publisher. Good news is always welcome.

Keith Yates - **keith_yates@awesomeauthors.org**

You might also want to check my blog for Updates and interesting info. keith-yates.awesomeauthors.org

About the Publisher

4Fun Publishing, a member of **BLVNP Incorporated**, 340 S. Lemon #6200, Walnut CA 91789, info@blvnp.com / legal@blvnp.com
NOTE: Due to the highly emotional reaction of some people to works of erotic fiction, any email sent to the above address that contains foul language or religious references is automatically deleted by our anti-spam software and will not be seen. All other communications are welcome.

DISCLAIMER

Please don't be stupid and kill yourself. This book is a work of FICTION. Do not try any new sexual practice that you find in this book. It is fiction and not to be confused with reality. Neither the author nor the publisher or its associates assume any responsibility for any loss, injury, death or legal consequences resulting from acting on the contents in this book. Every character in this book is over 18 years of age. The author's opinions are not to be construed as the opinions of the publisher. The material in this book is for entertainment purposes ONLY. Enjoy.

Keith
Yates

Coach's
Private Lessons

Hot Gay Erotica

Coach's Private Lessons
Hot Gay Erotica

By: Keith Yates

© **Keith Yates 2014**
ISBN: 978-1-62761-986-8

Chapter 1

TJ could not believe how much of a change being a college freshman was compared to a high school senior. He had been struggling all semester to keep up with classes, sports, friends and his girl friend. He had been a fantastic athlete in high school, but in college everyone seemed to be outstanding. In addition, the classes were much more of a struggle for him. He had to keep his grades up and since he was on a partial sports scholarship, he also had to perform well athletically.

Now in the past week, his long time high school girlfriend had dumped him; he had blown his Algebra test and screwed up in practice. Coach Walker had chewed him out royally and rightly so. TJ had not been concentrating. His mind had been on everything except his game. Coach had ordered him to start running laps and to not stop until given permission.

TJ was worried that he was going to get kicked off the team and lose his scholarship. His parents would be very disappointed in him. He would have to drop out as they could not afford the tuition without the scholarship.

TJ turned and saw that Coach Walker had stepped out of the locker room and was watching him. The man's blue eyes sent a shiver thru TJ. TJ always felt like those eyes were looking in his soul. TJ both admired Coach Walker and was also a little intimidated by the man. Chuck Walker was the picture of an alpha male. The man stood six feet two inches tall, had broad shoulders, a powerful chest, bulging arms, a trim narrow waist and powerful legs. His sandy blonde hair, deep blue eyes and roman jaw line left no doubt who was in charge.

"My office," Coach said as TJ ran back in his direction

TJ slowed down and started walking towards the locker room. His t-shirt clung to his sweaty chest. His brown hair was plastered to his scalp. He felt exhausted. TJ entered the Coach's Office and dropped down in a chair that was in front of the Coach's desk.

Walker moved to the desk and leaned against it as he looked down at the young man. The teenager's chest was still heaving. Walker half leaned and sat on the desk. He put the palms of his hands on the desk and studied TJ for a minute. He knew that the eighteen year old was an outstanding player. Walker himself had recruited the kid.

"TJ," Walker began, "For a few weeks now, you have not been performing up to your usual standard. I know you are a good player. I know what you can do on the court. Is there something going on? It is not unusual for guys to have a little trouble adjusting to college."

"I'm getting the hang of it," TJ said with his eyes fastened to the floor.

"Does that mean you are not having problems in your classes?" Coach asked.

"Um, not really," TJ said.

"They are harder than high school classes," Coach said his voice soft and projecting a tenderness that his frame did not.

"Yeah, they are more difficult than I thought they would be," TJ said his eyes finally lifting from the floor. He looked up and his eyes looked directly at Walker's basket. TJ swallowed and looked up at the Coach's body to his flat belly, broad powerful chest and finally to his bright blue eyes.

"You are a smart kid," Coach said. "You will get the hang of it. If you need help, I have a list of people willing to tutor."

"Um, thanks Coach," TJ said. TJ had a feeling that Coach's blue eyes were looking deep inside him.

"You have a girlfriend, right?" Coach asked.

"Um, sort of," TJ answered.

"Are things not going well?" Coach asked.

"Well," TJ began but hesitated. He felt embarrassed about being dumped.

"Guys and their high school girl friends often have a hard time that first semester at college," Coach said. "It is not unusual that the guy ends up getting dumped."

TJ's gaze had slid back down but he quickly looked back up at Coach Walker. "How did you know?"

Walker smiled, "It happens to all of us." Walker pushed off from the desk and squeezed TJ's shoulder before moving around behind his desk and taking a seat.

"It doesn't make sense to me," TJ said. "I thought things were fine."

Coach Walker chuckled and his lips curved up into a grin. "Hell boy it doesn't have to make sense when you are dealing with a girl. That is why I am still a single man."

"I guess," TJ said. He felt a little better that the Coach understood what he was going through.

"You know some of the tutors we have are nice looking girls," Coach pointed out. "You might be back in that saddle again before you know it."

"I'll keep that in mind," TJ said.

"Okay," Coach said. "Then hit the showers. You stink."

"Thanks Coach," TJ said.

"And keep you mind on your game," Coach added. "Keep it off of pussy when you are playing for me."

"Yes Sir," TJ said.

Walker watched TJ get up from the chair and pull his sweaty t-shirt over his head. Walker's eyes captured every inch of that young smooth chest. He checked out the athletic build of the young man. The skin was tan, smooth and clear. TJ's soft brown puppy eyes added to the kid's youthful appearance. If you did not know the boy was 18, you would think he was 15 or 16.

"Thanks for everything Coach," TJ said before turning and heading to the door.

Walker watched the young man walk to the door. His eyes traveled down of the strong shoulders, down the Plaines of the boy's back, down to the narrow waist and the clinging shorts. TJ's athletic butt was filling out the blue nylon fabric of the gym shorts perfectly.

"Kid has a hot ass," Walker thought. "He will have no problem finding a new girl friend."

Watching the athletic kid walk from the office caused the Coach to have some stirrings in his crotch that he had not felt for a while. His eyes drunk in every movement of that firm round jock butt as TJ walked to the door. His eyes slid over the athletic legs from the hem of the nylon shorts down to the white socks. Those legs were athletic, tan and had a very light dusting of blonde fuzz. Coach wondered if TJ ever fooled around with any of his jock buddies. "He might find another guy more fulfilling than a new girlfriend," Coach thought. Coach reached down and adjusted his growing manhood. His pants were getting a bit tight because of the thoughts he was having.

Walker's memory flashed back to his college days. He could remember how guys would help out their buddies. He could also remember how some of the Frats had worked that into their initiations. Coach would not mind being the one to initiate TJ. He felt his cock twitch again and begin to swell in his shorts. He had better get his mind off of this line of thought or he'd end up with a hard cock in no time.

TJ breathed a sigh of relief as he left the office. It had gone much better than he thought it would. He had really expected to get yelled at by the coach. He was glad the coach hadn't pressed him about his problems. It had been embarrassing enough to let Coach know he had been dumped. Telling Coach about not being able to jerk off in weeks would have been humiliating. He just never seemed to find a quiet place to masturbate. His roommate was always in the room. TJ wondered if the guy ever went to class. He had tried jerking his cock in a stall of the men's room, but thinking about Britney, his former girlfriend, did not get his juices flowing enough. His cock kept getting hard at all of the wrong times. It seemed to happen no matter what he was doing. He just needed to beat off really badly and that would help relieve his tension and get his mind back on the here and now.

TJ stopped in front of his locker. He tossed his sweaty shirt inside and kicked off his shoes. He then stripped down his nylon shorts. He tossed them into the locker and stood there in only his white athletic supporter. TJ could feel his cock strain to escape from the fabric pouch. He slid the jock strap down over his tan legs and threw it in atop his other clothes. TJ then picked up soap, shampoo and a towel and headed for the showers.

The showers were off by themselves in a separate little room in the locker room. There were 8 shower heads in the room 4 along each wall. There were no dividers between the shower heads, so when you looked in the door you could see exactly what every guy in the room had. TJ could still remember how nervous he had been the first time he had been expected to shower with the other guys. He was afraid that he wouldn't measure up to the other guys. But he soon learned that he was bigger than average. Or at least it seemed to be that way. TJ began thinking about his other teammates and seeing them all naked. He could still see them in his head with their athletic bodies and swinging cocks. His own cock jumped and twitched as he turned on the water. He began to shampoo his hair and rinse it out. Then he picked up the soap and began lathering up his body.

He did his arms running his hands up and down the lean muscles. He was feeling his young firm biceps. He was feeling the soft blonde hair on his forearms as he ran the soap up into his sweaty pits.

Then he began on his chest. He was running his soapy hands over his pecks. He was running His soapy fingers over his nipples. His nipples responded to the attention and grew hard as did his dick.

His hand slid down his smooth chest down over his flat belly down into his pubes. He ran the soap through his brown pubes and around under to his balls. He cupped his balls as his other hand began to slide up and down his hardening cock.

His slippery hand glided up and down the growing shaft. It felt so good to be stroking his cock. He needed so badly to blow his load. He looked around the room and knowing he was the only one left he began to pump up and down on his cock.

His cock was at full mast in no time. He rolled his cum filled balls around in his fingers as he pumped on his cock. It felt so nice to finally be able to work his meat.

TJ did not hear the coach close his office door and lock it. The coach heard water running in the showers. He wondered if TJ had left and forgot to turn the water all the way off or if he was still in there. He walked over to the shower room and stepped so he could look into the room.

He was quite surprised by the sight. TJ was standing there letting the water run over his naked body. His fist was wrapped around his rock hard cock. His other hand was cupping and fondling his balls. His fist was pumping up and down his boy meat fast and hard.

The coach watched the boy jacking his cock. Coach Watched as TJ was squeezing his balls as he stroked that rock hard young cock. It was quite a hot sight. His cock was growing hard inside his pants. The sight of the naked kid stroking his hard cock was sending surges into the Coach's own dick. TJ's smooth young body was glistening wet and trails of soap suds traveled down the tan skin. It was more than the cock in his pants could stand. The coach was fully hard and rubbing his big meat through his pants.

The coach knew he shouldn't be watching. He knew he should back away and let the young man pump his cock in private. However the desire in his cock was urging him to step into the shower with the boy. He wanted the kid to pump his big cock like he was pumping on his own. He wanted to feel those fingers working his own nuts over. Coach knew that stepping in there could end his career. It could cause him more problems than he cared to consider. If only, there was a way. A way he could have fun with the kid and keep the kid quiet about it. Hell the kid might even like the things running through the Coach's mind.

A plan began to form in the Coach's mind. A plan that made the man grin to himself. He was going to have fun with this kid and the kid was going to enjoy it too. Coach Walker took his hand off the swollen dick that was sliding down the leg of his pants. If anyone saw him, they would no instantly that he had a big hard-on and that he was very well endowed. He pulled out his phone with the megapixel camera. He pointed the camera at the young athletic boy and began snapping pictures. He took a couple shots of the boy pumping up and down. He took some of his full naked body and a couple of his face and of course the wonderfully hard young cock being stroked faster and more furiously than before. Coach's eyes and camera were glued onto that hot body. He watched and snapped as TJ masturbated. He caught images of the kid's fist pounding up and down that cock. He got pictures of the kid with his head thrown back with his eyes closed in pure pleasure.

"The boy sure is enjoying his jacking," coach thought as he worked on taking a couple of close ups of the boys hot round tan ass.

The coach zoomed in on that cock again focusing on it stepping as close as he dared and snapping a couple more shots. As he was taking the last one, TJ's cock exploded with a big hot load of cum.

TJ's load fired from his cock shooting out into the wall. Jet after jet of hot cum shot out and hit the wall. 3, 4, 5 huge jets of young hot white cum hit the wall and ran down. "Ahahahaha," TJ moaned in sexual bliss.

TJ let out a loud moan of pure pleasure as his hot jazz flew forth hitting the wall. He continued pumping making sure to pump every last drop of cum from his balls.

After the second or third shot, the coach backed away not wanting to get caught. His plan did not include being caught. At least not yet that is.

The Coach's own cock was rock hard from watching the show TJ had put on. The kid was hot and the Coach's cock knew what it wanted. The coach just hoped his plan would work. He hoped it wouldn't back fire.

TJ never noticed the coach watching him beat up and down on his meat. It had felt so good to shoot his load there in the locker room showers. He let the water wash the cum from his softening cock and the wall. He made sure there was no trace of his load left on the wall before grabbing his towel and heading back to his locker. He was standing before his locker totally naked when he saw the coach step out of his office.

"Doing okay TJ?" the Coach asked walking towards TJ.

TJ felt very nervous and exposed being totally naked with the Coach standing there fully dressed. The Coach even seemed to have a quirky smile on his face. He seemed to be looking over TJ's naked body.

He nervously answered, "Yeah sure Coach."

Walker could not keep his eyes from traveling over that young body. He could not keep from looking at the defined chest, very flat belly. He wanted to reach out and touch that smooth tan skin. He wanted to feel that firm round butt.

"That's good," Coach said moving past the kid. "Do you need a ride?"

"Um, no, I have it covered." TJ pulled his briefs from the locker and bent to put them on.

Smiling at that hot firm little ass as TJ bent over the Coach could not resist. He gave it a firm smack as he said, "Then you had better get a move on. Don't want to keep your ride waiting."

TJ jumped at the feeling of the hard smack on his ass. It stung just a little. The Coach had never done anything like that before, but then TJ had never been in this situation before. "Sure thing Coach."

The Coach had to work hard to control himself. His hand wanted to grab that hot smooth ass and squeeze those firm little cheeks. He wanted to slide his fingertips up and down that hairless crack. Wanted to pull those cheeks apart and expose that hot tight little pucker, and tease the boy's hot hole until he was begging for the Coach's cock. But the Coach controlled his desires and walked to the exit leaving TJ to get dressed. Coach new that maybe soon he would get to do just what he wanted with the boy. If his plan worked, he would have the boy begging for it.

Chapter 2

Chuck Walker had not been able to think of much the past few days but the boy he had found beating off in the school showers. Whenever he stepped into the locker room he had an image of that hot young athletic teen naked and dripping. He could see again the tan smooth skin, the hard young cock and the hot cum blowing from the head of that boy dick.

He watched his players changing into their workout clothes. He watched all of the lean athletic bodies. He watched them all, but his eyes kept going back to TJ. For some reason Coach had become fixated on that teen in particular. TJ was not as tall as some of the other guys. He was not as muscular as a few. However, there was something about the boy that drew Coach's attention to him. Maybe it was his puppy dog eyes that were very appealing. He did look younger than any of the other guys in the room. He looked more like 15 or 16 rather than 18. He was also not the most endowed boy. Coach believed that honor went to Lucas, but TJ had a nice looking piece of teenage flesh swinging between his legs. He definitely was above average.

Coach Walker had set up tutoring sessions for the teenager. He could tell the boy was having trouble adjusting to college life. It could be hard for some the first semester. Many did not make it and coach wanted to make sure TJ stayed around. He had some ideas brewing in his mind and having the boy dropping out was not an option.

He watched TJ sitting next to the attractive girl. He watched the two as they worked and he felt his cock plump at the thoughts that were brewing in his mind. "How is it going?" Coach asked.

"Just fine," Kelly answered. "TJ is one good student."

"Glad to hear that," Coach said and began massaging the soft skin and muscles on the back of TJ's neck. "We need this guy really badly."

"Don't worry," Kelly said "He will do just fine on the next exam."

"Great," Coach said and placed both hands on TJ and began massaging the kid's shoulders. He could feel how tight the boy was. He could also feel those tight muscles start to relax as his hands worked on them.

"Oh wow Coach," TJ breathed through the pleasure of the massage. "I am getting the hang of this now."

"Good," Coach said. "It is getting late though, so better finish next time. I have arranged for Kelly to be here after each practice."

"Um, thanks Coach," TJ said.

"You won't mind staying late will you?" Coach asked. His hands had moved from TJ's shoulders down to the firm biceps.

"Um, no not at all," TJ said.

"I'll see you next time then," Kelly said.

"I am glad you are willing to put in the extra effort," Coach said. His hands were now lightly massaging TJ's chest. "It shows your dedication.

"Um, thanks," TJ said. The teenage could feel his cock starting to grow. There was something about Coach's massage that was sending surges from TJ's balls into his teenage boner.

"Then hit the showers," Coach said.

"Sure," TJ said.

He slowly rose from the chair and grabbed his books. He held them in an attempt to hide his hard-on. He sure hoped that Coach had not noticed it. TJ could feel his ears burn with the thought of Coach Walker seeing the tent pole in his shorts.

The tent pole in TJ's shorts had not been unseen by Coach. He smiled to himself as he watched the teen leave the office. He watched that firm round boy butt move to the door and into the locker room. He watched as the boy walked out of his line of sight. Coach's own cock had grown. It was tenting out his pants. He rubbed his big hand over the front of his own shorts and squeezed his meaty cock. He could not wait to have that boy.

TJ quickly stripped off his clothes and headed to the showers. He tried to keep his cock out of sight just in case Coach stepped out of his office. He did not need Coach to see him walking through the locker room with a boner. The man would think he was perverted or something.

Coach Walker heard the water start running. He gave it another minute and then quietly slipped out of his office. He moved to the showers and watched as TJ began soaping up. He watched the sexy teenager wash his hair and he got out the digital camera and took picture after picture of that hot teenage body. He could even see that hot teenage boner sticking out from the patch of brown curls. He snapped a couple close-ups of that teenage boner. This digital camera took much better pictures than the one in Coach's cell phone. He could not help but get even hornier as he photographed the boy. He watched as TJ began soaping up that teenage bone. He watched as the boy began fondling his almost hairless balls. He watched and he snapped picture after picture.

Coach's own cock was just as hard as TJ's. It was throbbing to be released from the tight shorts. It was leaking a constant stream of pre-cum into the Coach's jock strap. He pushed down the front of his shorts and pulled the jock strap to one side to let his big thick man cock out. It swung free pointing right at TJ. It was almost like the piss slit was an eye and it had spotted exactly what it wanted. It wanted that hot tan jock boy. It wanted that hot mouth. It wanted that hot tight virgin butt. Coach let the camera hang around his neck and he fondled his own cock as he watched TJ masturbate.

TJ's eyes were closed as he stroked his raging boner. His fist was wrapped around that turgid member and was pumping from the wet base to the blood engorged head. His brown little nipples were erect as he fondled and stroked his raging teen boner. Water cascaded down over his lean athletic body. Water flowed over the round smooth muscular butt and down his tan legs.

"Oh oh," he breathed as he felt his balls drawing up. He felt his teenage boyhood getting ready to squirt his juice. He felt the surge of electricity flood thru him.

Walker's cock was rock hard as he stood there in the shadows out of sight and watched that hot teenager pumping that teenage cock. Walker's own fist was wrapped around his manhood stroking from the dark sandy pubes to the fat purple head. He wanted to push that teenage jock down to his knees. He wanted to slap that cute young face with his fat cock snake. He wanted those lips around his cock. He wanted that cute little mouth to be filled to capacity with hot hard man dick. He wanted that kid to choke on his pole. He wanted to shoot his cum right down that kid's throat. He wanted TJ to swallow a hot thick load of man juice. He wanted it and he was going to make it happen.

"Ahahahaha," TJ moaned as his cock jerked and squirted forth a load of teenage sperm. White milky jets of cum blasted from that teenage boner and hit the shower wall. His hot white gizz slid down the wall. "Oh fuck," TJ moaned.

"Oh shit," Walker breathed as he almost came. He quickly stepped back when he saw TJ's eyes open. He moved back further getting out of sight. He still had his hand wrapped around his rock hard man pole. He had strands of pre-cum stretching from the piss slit towards the locker room floor.

Walker could not get his big thick cock back into the snug athletic supporter. He moved into his office and was willing his cock to go down. He wanted to blow his load but he was not ready to be caught by that horned up teenager. He would remain in control of the situation. He would have the upper hand and he would be making that teenage jock drop to his knees and suck this big cock.

Coach Walker heard the bare feet moving from the showers to the lockers. He heard TJ getting dressed. When he heard it and he finally managed to get his cock back into his shorts. He knew that there would be an obvious bulge, but he could not help that. He was a well endowed man and maybe the kid would even be intrigued to see the bulge in his shorts.

TJ pulled on his white briefs. And he was just about to step into shorts when he noticed Coach Walker stepped out of his office. He admired this man more than any of the other college instructors. He was so damn handsome and built like a professional athlete. The sandy hair, blue eyes, broad shoulders and muscular chest made him a very hot looking man. TJ had been noticing more and more lately how guys looked. He had been noticing more and more how their bodies looked. He had not been able to stop himself from checking out guys in the locker room. He had been fascinated by a couple of his teammates who had hairy chests. It made his own totally smooth chest feel naked.

"Doing okay TJ?" Coach asked turning towards the young man.

"Sure coach," TJ said and then glanced down and noticed the large bulge in the front of Coach's shorts. He had always noticed that Coach seemed to be sporting quite a hefty basket, but TJ noticed for the first time just how interesting that basket was.

"Well, get a move on," Coach said. "Shake that ass."

"Yes Sir," TJ said and quickly finished getting dressed. TJ stepped out of the locker room and found Coach standing there.

"It is a nice night isn't it TJ," Walker said.

"Um, sure Coach," TJ said.

"I just want to tell you, that I am glad the tutoring seems to be helping."

"It sure is Coach," TJ said. "Thanks so much for setting that up."

"No problem," Coach said and slid his arm around TJ's shoulders as they walked. "I always take care of my players. That is what we do. We take care of each other. I take care of you and you take care of my needs and I need a winning team."

"Oh you will get that coach," TJ said. TJ could feel the heat of the man coming thru his thin t-shirt. He could feel the strong fingers on his shoulder and then his chest as Coach pulled him closer. TJ could not stop a surge of sexual power flow into his cock. He felt it growing as the Coach walked with him. He felt it and he felt his ears and neck burn with the embarrassment. He hoped that in the dusk that Coach could not see the blush crept up his neck.

"That is good TJ," Coach said. "I am glad you are a kid that knows how to play ball."

"I am Coach," TJ said.

"I'm parked over here," Coach said. "Do you need a ride?"

"No," TJ said stopping and turning. He glanced down again and could still see the obvious bulge in Coach's shorts. "My dorm is just over there."

"Okay," Coach said. See you at practice." Coach walked passed TJ and as he did he reached out and planted a hard slap on that hot tight little bottom. He felt the kid jump in surprise and smiled. He wanted to spank that hot ass and then he wanted to do so much more to it.

Coach decided he needed something better than a digital camera. He decided he needed something that he would not have to hold, so he stopped by a computer store that an old college buddy owned. He decided to make an investment in TJ that he was going to make pay-off one way or another.

What Coach needed cost quite a bit, but he knew it was going to be worth it. The new electronic gadgets were going to pay off for the man in a number of ways.

Walker had TJ stay after practice again. The tutoring was going well and Walker knew just what he would do while TJ was getting tutored by Kelly. By the time the tutoring session was over, Coach had finished setting up his new electronic toys.

Coach sat down at his laptop and watched the screen. The cameras were working perfectly. "Thank you Ted," Coach Thought to his old college buddy. The man had known exactly what Coach had needed.

Coach watched as TJ's naked body stepped into the showers. His tan skin and soft cock filled the screen as Coach sat back and pushed his shorts and jock strap down. He started slowly stroking himself as he watched. The boy wasted no time and getting his naked body lathered up. He wasted no time in beginning to masturbate that teenage bone.

Coach watched the hot teenager and slowly stroked up and down on his own tool. Coach's fist slid from the dark sandy colored pubes to the fat head. He watched the computer screen and slowly stroked. He rubbed his thumb over the purple head and smeared his pre-cum all around it.

TJ's soapy fist once again found his teenage boner. His soapy hand slid easily up and down that hot and rock hard young cock. He fondled his cum filled balls with his other hand. He couldn't help himself

"Oh fuck," Walker breathed. "I got to have that." He quickly began cleaning up. He was going to find a way to have that boy's ass.

TJ was bent over tying his shoe when Walker stepped out of his office. He walked over to the hot jock boy. "Need a ride TJ?"

"Um, no thanks Coach," TJ said. "I'm good."

"Your ass certainly is," Coach thought but said "Okay, see you next practice." Then he reached back and slapped the left cheek of that hot little ass. He couldn't wait to have his hands on that firm round butt. Coach could not wait to part those two cheeks and inspect that tight little virgin hole. He was definitely going to enjoy this semester and he had an idea that young TJ would end up finding this his best semester ever.

TJ jumped at the physical contact. The slaps to the ass that Coach had been giving him kept surprising TJ. He guessed it was something guys from Coach's generation did, but TJ found it a bit odd. Plus the slaps stung. That one Coach had planted on his bare ass had left a red hand print on his butt.

TJ watched Coach leave and then quickly followed the man out. He could not stop thinking about the masculine body and the bulge he had once again noticed in Coach's shorts. He wondered just how big the man's cock was.

"Knock it off," TJ thought to himself as he walked to his dorm. "You keep thinking like that and you will end up doing something queer."

Chapter 3

The past two weeks of TJ's freshman year had moved slowly for the teen. He was barely keeping up with his classes and he had Coach Walker paying more attention to him. He felt like Coach had taken a special interest in him.

Coach had made TJ stay late after every practice. He had been providing a tutor to help TJ with the class he had been having trouble with. The tutoring had helped him understand the subject better, but the tutor made him uncomfortable. The girl was a graduate student and she always seemed to be looking at TJ like a piece of meat. She would often get to close and touch him when she did not need too. TJ knew he needed the help, so he did not complain to Coach Walker.

Thanks to the tutoring, TJ's grades had improved a little. Another benefit of staying after practice was he got some alone time in the showers. By the time the tutoring was over, all of the other guys had left. He could strip down and masturbate without worrying about his roommate. In fact TJ had noticed that his cock seemed to be developing a mind of its own. He seemed to be popping a boner more and more often in the locker room. He seemed to be associating that room with his sexual pleasure.

"You really seem to understand this so much better," Kelly, TJ's tutor, said.

"Thanks," TJ said. "You do a better job of explaining it than Mr. Parker."

"You are so sweet," she said and put her hand on TJ's bare leg and squeezed it.

"So he is doing better than," Coach Walker said coming up behind the two who had been using his office for their tutoring sessions.

TJ felt Kelly pull her hand away from his bare leg. He felt a blush creep up his neck at having been caught being felt up by a girl.

"Yes, he is," Kelly said.

"That is very good news," Coach Walker said. "We need him on my team." Coach Walker moved behind TJ and put his hands on the teenager's shoulders. He began to massage the muscles.

"We will definitely keep his grades up so he can keep playing," Kelly said confidently.

"So same time Thursday," Coach said as he continued to massage TJ's shoulders.

"For sure," she said as she gathered up her books and papers.

"Thanks Kelly," TJ said.

"See you Thursday," she said and winked at him.

TJ felt his face blush again as she left the room.

"Go hit the shower," Coach said. "Then come back and see me. I want to talk a bit."

"Sure Coach," TJ said.

As TJ walked to his locker, he could feel his cock beginning to grow. He had been masturbating in the shower after every practice and it looked like his cock was in need of more attention. These days it seemed like he would get boned up at the strangest times. Sometimes it was in the locker room when the guys were changing. Sometimes he would get boned while being lectured by Coach Walker. It seemed to be happening more and more frequently.

TJ stopped in front of his locker. He pulled his sweaty T-shirt off and then popped the lock. He tossed the shirt inside and then slid down his shorts and jock strap. He got his stuff for the shower and headed that way. He could feel his cock growing harder and harder as he walked.

"Shit the damn thing has gotten use to be beating it off in the shower," he said to himself as he made his way through the rows of lockers to the showers.

"TJ," the Coach said. The Coach was standing a little behind and off to the side in his office doorway.

"Fuck," he said under his breath as he tried to hold the towel to hide his growing dick. "Um yeah, Coach?"

"Do not take too long in the shower," Coach said. "I have plans tonight."

"Oh of course not Coach," TJ said hoping that his cock wasn't showing as he only half turned to look in the coach's direction.

Coach couldn't help smiling as he had turned away. He had seen the kid trying to hide his young hard cock. Today seemed like as good a day as ever to put his little plan into action. He just hoped that it wouldn't back fire on him.

TJ stepped into the shower his cock still swinging in front of him. It seemed his cock liked being hard and almost being caught walking through the locker room with a rock hard rod added to the excitement. TJ didn't know what was going on. A part of him seemed to find it exciting and erotic being naked in the locker room sporting a woody.

TJ shampooed his brown hair and let the water rinse the soap down over his lean tan body. He soaped up his body. He was washing his sweaty pits and running the soap through his brown pubes. Soapy fingers were fondling his heavy balls and running up and down his hard shaft.

He wanted to jack off, but he didn't know if he had the time. Plus what if Coach got impatient and came looking for him. What if he found TJ in the shower with a boner and his fist pumping up and down on it?

TJ's cock gave a jump at the thought. Fuck, but he found it all too exciting. He had to get these thoughts out of his mind. He just had to find a new girlfriend. Maybe he should start flirting back with Kelly. She was pretty, but for some reason TJ was not being turned on by her. He was sure he just needed to find a girl that was more his type.

He finished his shower and hurried back to his locker. For the most part, his cock had finally softened.

TJ pulled on a pair of blue briefs, a pair of shorts, and a tee shirt. He sat down on the wooden bench and pulled his Nikes on before he headed to the Coaches office.

He found Coach sitting behind his desk in a Navy wife beater. His hair was damp and the shirt looked fresh. Coach must have used the time while TJ was showering to make use of the personal shower in a corner of the coach's office.

TJ couldn't help but admire the man's athletic body. Coach had broad shoulders and a powerful chest tapering down to a narrow waist. The big biceps emphasized the fact that he took the time to keep himself in shape. TJ knew from watching the Coach during practices that his legs were just as well muscled as the rest of him. The man was definitely an athlete and had the body to prove it. TJ liked the way Coach's chest hair showed around the edges of the wife beater. It looked darker than the well trimmed sandy colored hair on his head. It seemed to emphasize Coaches masculinity.

"Good TJ. Come in and have a seat," Coach said looking up from the laptop he had been concentrating on.

TJ took a seat and looked nervously at the coach. He knew he was going to get a lecture and just hoped he wasn't going to be kicked off the team.

"I have had a talk with some of your teachers," Coach began. "It seems that they are experiencing the same thing that I am. Your mind does not seem to be on the subject at hand. You seem to not be able to concentrate."

"I am trying," TJ started explaining. "I, I, just seem to get, um distracted easily. Kelly is really helping. My grades are starting to improve."

"Are you having problems at home?" Coach asked.

"Oh no everything at home is just fine," TJ said.

"Well, then I believe I know what your problem is." Coach said a twinkle in his eye.

"You do?" TJ asked puzzled.

"Yes," Coach said. "It is something we must address. We cannot let it continue."

"What? What do you think my problem is," TJ asked.

"Well, it appears from what I have seen that you are too fucking horny for your own good." The coach said his voice taking on a more firm and disapproving tone.

TJ did not know what to say. He had never expected Coach to say this. This was not what he wanted to hear. He could feel his face beginning to burn with embarrassment "Coach I do not know what you were told but..."

"TJ do not tell me it isn't true." The Coaches voice taking on a stern tone. "You have broken several school rules to satisfy your sexual desires."

Sexual desires. What was he talking about? He hadn't broken any school rules. TJ voiced this to Coach.

"Now TJ don't give me that line of bull shit," Coach said. "Or do you think your pleasuring of yourself in the shower is approved by the school?"

TJ felt his stomach drop, felt the redness creeping hire up his neck as he realized the Coach knew. "I... I, I, don't know what you are talking about."

Coach's eyes seemed to burn as he looked TJ over. TJ thought they were burning with anger. Little did he know that the fire inside Coach was not anger but a long awaited desire for the young man.

"Don't give me that shit TJ," Coach said. The Coach's voice had risen as he started phase one of his plan. "I have all the proof I need."

"Proof?" TJ asked wondering what kind of proof Coach could have. Had one of the other teammates came back and saw him in the shower stroking?

"Yes!" Coach said as he turned the lap top around so TJ could see the screen.

TJ's eyes bugged out as he saw what was on the screen. There was a picture of him in the shower stroking his cock. His soapy hand was wrapped around his rock hard boner.

TJ's mouth went dry. He didn't know what to say. He was afraid, dreading what might happen if anyone else found it. His team mates would never let him forget this. If Coach told the Dean, then they would tell his parents. Fuck it, but he would be screwed or die of embarrassment.

"Do you have nothing to say for yourself?" Coach asked.

"I, I, I was just taking a shower...I was just washing myself." TJ knew no one would believe that, but he had to try something.

"Is that so?" Coach said. His muscular arm was reaching around so he could hit the arrow key. The picture changed to another pick of TJ stroking. Coach hit the key again and the picture changed again. Again Coach hit the key and the picture changed.

Coach hit the key several times until the picture of TJ shooting his cum from his cock and hitting the wall was on the screen. His mouth went even drier. His face was burning red from embarrassment. He felt like he might be sick.

"Okay, Okay, I...I just did it that one time." TJ began explaining. He was talking fast hoping Coach would believe him. He was hoping to get it over with fast. "I had just been dumped. The bitch had gotten me all excited and then dumped me. I couldn't do it in my dorm room because my stupid roommate is always there. He never even seems to go to class. It was the only place I could find. Please, please don't tell anyone else. It was only that one time. I won't do it again."

"Just the one time, hmm?" Coach said as he turned the lap top back around. "You won't do it again." Coach's voice said that he didn't believe a word.

"Only the once," TJ said trying to convince him. "I promise it won't happen again."

Coach was bringing up another file as he said, "How the hell can I believe you won't do it again when you are lying to me right now." Coach's voice had taken on the stern tone again. "You sit there telling me it only happened once. That you promise you won't do it again. How can I believe you won't do it again when you are lying about it only happening that one time?"

"I, I'm not lying coach," TJ stuttered. "Honest only the once."

The Coach slapped the desk hard with his hand making TJ jump startled by the sound echoing in the room. "Stop your fucking lying. Stop it right now. You fucking little horn ball. Sitting there and lying to my face."

Time for Phase two the Coach thought as he turned the laptop back around and let TJ see the screen. TJ was shocked and just about fell out of his chair. It wasn't just a picture of him stroking his hard cock filling the screen. This time it was a video of him beating his meat. His hand moved up and down his shaft. His fingers fondled his balls as he stroked. His head was leaning back and his eyes were closed in sexual pleasure. TJ watched his body tense up. He watched as his cock erupted and his cum shot out. TJ lost the ability to speak as he watched himself jerking off. He had no idea how Coach had gotten this. He had no idea what he was going to do.

"As you can see the video has a time and date stamp down there in the bottom right corner." Coach knew he had the boy by the balls and now it was time to take it all the way. Under the desk his own cock was throbbing and leaking pre cum with excitement. His tight white jockeys were getting wet with his cock juices.

I have two other files on this laptop with different date stamps. "It seems you have been using my locker room as your personal jack off room."

"How? Where? What?" TJ tried to ask where and how he had gotten this but the words would not come out.

"You see TJ," Coach said a smirk on his face. "These days, digital video cameras are so small that they can be easily missed. Especially by a horny boy who is only thinking about stroking his cock until it explodes all over the shower wall."

TJ did not think his face could get any hotter but it was. Fuck, he hated this. He hated feeling like this. Seeing his own cock shooting onto the wall and floor of the shower he finally pulled his eyes from the screen and looked at the floor in shame.

"Tired of looking at yourself?" Coach asked. "Or would you like to see one of the other videos?"

"What, what are you going to do with them?" TJ asked his voice soft and desperate.

"Well, as a teacher it is my duty to take this to the Dean and let him set some sort of discipline." Coach leaned back and raised his hands behind his head. He could feel his cock throbbing under the desk. "But as your one of my players, maybe we should take care of this situation between the two of us."

TJ looked up hope beginning to grow in his gut. He looked up into the coaches blue eyes. TJ Looked at the tufts of arm pit hair showing as the coach leaned back in his chair. The big biceps bulged as he looked directly at TJ.

TJ felt his cock twitch. "Fuck not now," TJ thought.

"What do you think TJ want us to handle this between just the two of us?" Coach asked.

"Yes please," TJ stammered. "Please Coach don't take it any further. I admit that I have been doing that but I will stop. It doesn't have to go any further. Please Coach." TJ was practically begging.

"Well, I will still have to set some sort of punishment. Something that fits the crime as it were."

"Sure Coach," TJ said. He could feel the knot in his stomach loosen a little. "I will be happy to run more laps or even clean the locker room and equipment or whatever you want."

"Hmmm I don't think running laps is really a fitting punishment."

"Then what?" TJ asked.

"Well, it seems as if it should be something that fits the crime," Coach said. He could feel his cock straining against the fabric of his shorts.

"Whatever you think is right Coach. Just as long as this doesn't have to go any further than between us."

"When I was a year or so younger than you," Coach began. "My father caught me smoking and cigarette smoking was against the rules, so as my punishment my father forced me to smoke a whole pack. I had to smoke one right after the other. It made me as sick as a dog and I have never wanted one since. Even the thought makes my stomach churn."

TJ did not know where Coach was going. Was he going to be forced to smoke until he began throwing up? He didn't understand what one thing had to do with the other.

"I think your crime should be treated the same way," Coach said. "You like jacking off so much that you have been doing it in my locker room. Then I think I will take a page from my father's book and give you what you want."

Coach slid his chair back and stood up moving around the desk. He did not try and hide the raging hard on he had. His cock was thick and pushing out the front of his shorts. There was no way TJ could miss the boner.

TJ's eyes locked on the bulge in Coach's shorts as he moved to the front of his desk. He leaned against the desk his crotch eye level with TJ.

"You like jacking on cock so much," Coach said. "Then jack on mine."

"What?" TJ said stunned. "No way...No fucking way."

"You said you wanted me to handle this. That you didn't want me to take these issues to the Dean. Now you're already giving me trouble."

"Coach, you're joking right," TJ said. "I mean, I may jack off, but I am not queer. I ain't going to stroke another guy's cock."

"YES you are," Coach said in a commanding tone. "Your fucking hand had better be around my cock in the next few seconds or all deals are off. I will take these images to the Dean and have him deal with this situation. I am sure he will have to call your parents in and show them what their boy has been doing at school. Hell it may have to even go before the board."

TJ could feel his heart sinking at the thought of his parents seeing him jacking off. Not to mention the Dean and the board. Fuck, he was so screwed.

"Soon everyone will know what you have been doing. How easy do you think it will be for you to land a new girl friend then? Not to mention what your teammates will think of you."

He knew it was all true. He would be the laughing stock of the school. No girls would date him. The team would tease and torment him forever. He had little choice. He would have to - have to stroke Coach. TJ's own cock jumped at the thought of touching Coach's man post.

"Now get to work on my cock!" The command in the Coach's voice left little room for argument.

Looking up at the man TJ sighed. "Is there no other way?"

"NO!" Coach said. His tone left no doubt that TJ had one option.

TJ reached up and began rubbing the thick meat through the fabric of his shorts. He could feel the heat of the swollen man meat. Feel the wetness of the pre cum on the fabric of the shorts.

"Fucking do it right," Coach ordered. "Take my fucking cock out and wrap your fingers around it and fucking stroke me properly."

TJ slowly lowered Coach's shorts and jockey briefs revealing his large man cock. It was thick and long had to be close to 2 or 3 inches longer than TJ's own cock. Not to mention thick and pre cum was leaking from the big mushroom head.

Coach let the shorts slide down his legs and to the floor. His cock throbbed as TJ finally reached out and took it in his hand. He could feel the boy's hand shake a bit as he grasp the rock hard slab of meat.

TJ squeezed the thick meat testing the thickness slowly gliding his hand up the long shaft. His fingers brushing the rim of the head before he slid them back down to feel the thick dark pubes brushing against his fingers.

"That's it kid, stroke your Coach. Stroke me just like you were stroking yourself in the shower."

TJ began stroking Coach Walker. His hand was slowly gliding up and down the thick shaft. His fingers were rubbing the head as he stroked. He felt the pre cum oozing onto his fingers as he stroked that thick dick. The juice was making his hand slide a little easier up and down the thick long man pole.

"That's it come on stroke me like you mean it. Don't forget about my balls. Do me really well or else."

TJ reached up with his other hand and began rolling those big cum filled nuts around in his fingers. He felt the hairy wrinkly sack in his fingers. He worked the nuts with one hand and the big dick with the other.

"Uhah does that feel good," Coach moaned.

As TJ stroked the Coach faster and harder squeezing that big Fuck pole, he noticed his own cock was rock hard in his shorts. He realized he had pre cum oozing from his own cock.

The Coach moaned louder as TJ picked up his pace again. TJ's hand was gliding up and down Coach's engorged cock. TJ's fingers were fondling Coach's big balls. It felt so good. The boy was a good cock stroker. He had probably had lots of practice.

Coach reached down and grabbed TJ's hand holding it still on his cock. "Strip off your clothes," he ordered.

TJ looked stupidly up at him as if not understanding the simple command.

"I said," Coach said louder than before. "Take off your fucking clothes and do it now."

"What, what for?" TJ questioned.

Coach grabbed the kid under his arms and pulled him to his feet. "Don't ask why you little horn ball. Just do as you're told. Now get them off."

TJ slowly pulled his shirt off and then kicked off his shoes before lowering his shorts and underwear. His young cock was rock hard and it slapped his belly as he freed it from his underwear.

"Humm, looks like maybe this isn't reducing your desire to jack off." Coach's eyes took in the rock hard young cock as it slapped TJ's belly.

In Coach's opinion, TJ was one of the best looking players on the team. The brown hair and those brown puppy dog eyes were very appealing to Coach. Plus he loved TJ's lean tan body. The muscles beginning to develop under that smooth skin. TJ also had small brown nipples on his smooth developing chest.

"Now get back to work on my cock," Coach ordered.

TJ grasped the man's big thick rod and began stroking again. He pumped it up and down his hand was gliding up the thick shaft. His fingers were rubbing the mushroom head. He twisted his hand on the down stroke. His other hand had returned to Coaches nuts. The two stood there facing each other as TJ stroked Coach's thick dong. Coach could tell that the boy was enjoying stroking a hot man dick. He knew TJ was going to enjoy the next step even more.

"Oh yeah, that's it TJ your doing a good job," he said. "Now it's time for the second part of your punishment. Now you're going to suck this big hot man cock."

TJ's fist stopped in mid stroke. He was stunned by the words. They couldn't be right. The Coach hadn't said that. It was just not true what he had heard.

Coach had his hand on TJ's shoulder pushing him back down into the chair he had been sitting in. TJ watched as Coach's big cock swung back and forth before him.

"Go on taste my dick. Suck me TJ. Suck your Coach's cock."

TJ was breathing easier now that Coach wasn't pushing the whole thing down his throat. He slowly worked his tongue around the big head tasting the juices leaking from it. He was so surprised that it didn't taste bad. It was a little salty and bitter, but not really bad. He began to slowly work his mouth up and down on the thick meat.

"WATCH THOSE FUCKING TEETH!" The coach shouted when TJ's teeth grazed the sensitive head.

TJ tried being more careful as he worked his lips up and down on the big thick man cock. He was easily taking about half of the thick monster cock into his mouth and trying to take a little more.

His own cock was rock hard and dripping pre cum onto the chair he was sitting on. He could not believe he was actually enjoying sucking on this hot cock, but he must be if his cock was harder than he could ever remember it being in the past.

TJ reached down and began to stroke himself as he sucked down further onto the Coach's cock.

"Who the fuck said you could do that?" Coach asked.

TJ continued sucking and stroking himself. He couldn't answer the question and say he was fucking horny and so hard that his cock almost hurt.

Coach reached down and took TJ's hand off the boy cock. "You don't seem to understand that we are trying to break you of that habit. You only get to stroke that cock of yours at the right time and I will tell you when that is." Coach let go of the hand he had pulled off the kids cock. He had begun to slowly move his hips in and out slightly and slowly fucking the kid's hot wet mouth.

TJ waited a minute or two, but couldn't help himself. His hand returned to his cock and he began stroking again.

Coach stepped back pulling his hard cock from the boy's mouth. "I told you to stop that."

"But Coach, it's so hard. I have to," TJ said still stroking it. He needed to cum so bad. He had to stroke himself.

Coach moved over to a shelf and grabbed a jump rope. He moved behind TJ and grabbed both of his hands. He looped the rope through the chair and around TJ's wrists. He tied TJ's arms behind his back. The boy didn't put up much of a struggle. He must have known it was fruitless.

"Coach, please don't. I need to stroke myself. It hurts. I am so hard."

"Are you saying that sucking my cock has made you fucking hornier than ever before?" Coach asked.

"Well, no, no not that. It, it has just been a, a while since my last um cum."

"Well, if you do a good job on my cock, then maybe, just maybe I will let you beat that hard young cock of yours."

Coach stepped back up to TJ his still rock hard man cock glistening in the light. It was still slick with his pre cum and TJ's spit.

TJ did not have to be told. He opened his mouth and let coach slide his cock back in. This time when he felt the head hit his throat, he swallowed and was able to take more of that big meat.

"OOOHHH YEEEAAAH that is it kid. MMMMMM you do that so gooooood."

TJ worked his mouth harder and faster up and down the cock in front of him. He sucked it harder and faster. He needed to satisfy the coach so he could satisfy his own cock.

Coach watched the naked youth sucking him. Looking down at the hot young man working his lips up and down his thick cock was a turn on to the older man. Reaching down he ran a big hand over that smooth chest and played with the hard little nipples. Couch loved the sight of his thick dick sliding between TJ's cute lips. He loved the feeling of those teenage lips massaging his bull dick. He would never grow tired of having that tongue teasing his fat mushroom head.

TJ moaned as the coach teased his nipples. He liked the feeling. He never knew it could feel so good to have his nipples played with like this. TJ's cock twitched between his legs. The pre cum was flowing steadily from the head. It throbbed and jumped straining for a release that was so badly needed. Coach reached down and took the kid's cock in his hand. He held it, felt the wetness on the head and rubbed it up and down.

TJ moaned around the cock in his mouth. It felt so good having Coach stroke him. Having another hand on his cock, felt amazing to the horny teen. It was wonderful. This was the first time for the eighteen year old to have another guy fondle him. His former girlfriend had touched it, but it had felt nothing like this. The Coach was giving him more pleasure than TJ had ever gotten from Brittany.

Coach stroked the kid. The young cock felt hot and warm in his hand. The young juice was making it nice and slick. Using an over hand grip he pumped up and down on the hot smooth cock.

"That's it TJ, suck me good and maybe I will stroke you off," Coach said giving the cock in his hand a firm squeeze.

TJ moaned again wanting to be stroked and he sucked ever harder and faster on Coach's cock.

Coach pumped faster and harder. It didn't take long before he knew the kid was going to cum and he slowed his pace. Slowed it to where his hand was just barely moving. TJ had been so close. He thought he was going to get his release, but then coach slowed his stroking. He whimpered in need. Trying to wordlessly beg for Coach to fucking jack him off and make him cum.

"Want to shoot so bad don't you kid," Coach said. "Well, as soon as you get all my cock down your throat, then I might let you cum."

TJ began sucking harder and working his mouth steadily down the last couple inches that he hadn't managed to suck in yet. Soon he had it all in his mouth had every inch of thick meat buried down his throat. His nose was in the thick dark pubes as he deep throated Coach.

"AAAAAAAHHHHHH yes finally," Coach moaned. "I knew you could do it."

Coach grabbed TJ's head with his large hands. He tangled his fingers into the soft brown hair and held on as he began to slowly fuck the teen's mouth. He pushed in and out. His cock was oozing pre cum and getting closer and closer to shooting.

TJ felt the cock in his mouth grow even thicker and longer. He couldn't have believed it could get any bigger, but it was. He felt the balls against his chin tighten up as the first jet of hot juice shot right down his throat.

Coach pulled back and let the boy suck on the head as he shot into the hot mouth. Jet after jet of hot cum shot into TJ's mouth. TJ discovered that it tasted good. He liked the feeling of it on his tongue and the warm liquid slid easily down his throat. There was just so much of it. He couldn't keep up with it. The cum began running out of his lips. He could feel it leaking out and dripping down off his chin down onto his chest and oozing all over his neck.

Coach moaned loudly as each hot jet of cum left his cock and went into the boy's mouth. It was the best orgasm he'd had in years. It seemed to last and last, but really only went on for a few moments.

Coach Walker couldn't believe how good TJ was. The kid was a star athlete and one fucking good cock sucker. "OH yes TJ that was great for your first time," Coach said pulling his cock from the kid's mouth. TJ licked the cum from his lips. He could still feel it dripping from his chin. His own cock still yearned for release.

"You did really well," Coach said rubbing the boy's bare shoulder.

"Um, then, can I cum now?" TJ asked hopefully.

Coach looked down at the boy's erection. The cock was rock hard sticking out and still dripping with pre cum. It had formed a good sized little pool on the floor.

"Looks like that young cock of yours is ready to explode isn't it?" Coach said.

"OH yes it is Coach. Please untie me so I can jack off."

"Is that what you want to jack yourself off?" Coach asked in a teasing tone.

"Oh yes I need to cum so bad," TJ said.

Coach reached down between the boys legs and wrapped his hand around that hard rod. He ran his thumb over the head which was slick with juice.

TJ moaned as he felt the hand grasp his cock. He moaned even louder when Coach ran his thumb over his sensitive head.

"Please, please," TJ begged. "Please let me cum. Let me jack off Coach please."

Coach slowly stroked the cock in his hand looking at TJ. "How does that feel?"

"OH so good Coach. Please stroke it faster. Please stroke it harder."

"Is that what you want for me to beat you off?" coach asked.

"Yes" was all TJ said.

"Well, all you need to do is ask," Coach said.

"Please faster coach please." TJ said almost whimpering with the feelings of frustration at coach's slow hand movement.

"Exactly what is it you want?" Coach asked.

"OOHH Fuck Coach please stroke me. Stroke me fast and hard. Fucking jerk me off now. I need it so bad I want to cum."

Coach tightened his grip on the hard cock and began to really stroke the kid. His hand squeezed firmly as it slid up and down the shaft. He twisted his hand left and right as he stroked. He would rub the head every time he stroked up on the shaft.

TJ's moans grew louder and in only a minute he was blowing his load. The first jet of hot white cum was shooting out and hitting the front of Coach's desk. The rest of the cum was landing on the floor adding to the puddle of boy jizz.

TJ sat gasping as the last of his juice dripped from his cock. His body was covered in new sweat and the Coach's cum. Coach was still stroking him getting the last of the load from him. His thumb rubbing TJ's overly sensitive head was driving him nuts.

"OH fuck Coach," TJ finally managed to say. "I don't think I have ever cum so hard or much before."

Releasing TJ's softening cock Coach said, "You did make quite a mess. Looks like part of your punishment will have to be to clean this up."

"You will not tell anyone about any of this or my jacking off in the showers will you Coach?"

"I think we will keep this between just the two of us," Coach said. "Hopefully you won't be jacking off in the showers anymore."

"Oh no, I have learned my lesson about that," TJ said.

"Good. Now I expect your game to get back on track and for your grades to improve. I want your Algebra grade back up to where it was."

"Oh I will try my hardest to do better on the court and in the classroom too."

Coach reached down and grabbed his shorts and underwear. He pulled them up his long hairy legs letting his limp cock settle inside them. He adjusted himself so his thick meat was hanging properly. He noticed TJ watching him as he pulled his clothes back on and him adjust his cock.

"Um, Coach, can you untie me now?" he asked.

"Sure," Coach said. "I think we are done for today."

Coach released TJ's hands. TJ rubbed his wrists where the rope had cut into them just a little. Then he wiped some of the cum from his face with his hand.

"You're quite the cum covered little cock sucker aren't you," Coach said grinning down at TJ.

"Well, I guess I should take another shower," TJ said.

"Well first you have to clean up the mess you made on my desk and floor," Coach said.

TJ looked at the large pool of cum on the floor and the cum on the front of the desk. He still could not believe he had shot so far or so much. He did not understand why it had felt so good. He did not understand how he had enjoyed it so much. TJ knew he was going to have to think about this whole incident and try and figure out his feelings. Maybe it was just that he was so horny. That had to be it.

Coach picked up TJ's blue briefs and tossed them to him. "Use that to clean up the mess," Coach instructed the cum covered jock. "Then you can hop in my shower to clean up.

TJ hated to have to use his own underwear to wipe up the cum, but he knew that this was all part of Coach's punishment. It would not be the first time TJ had gone without underwear. "Okay, thanks Coach," TJ said.

Coach watched the boy get down on the floor and start wiping up the mess he had made. Coach enjoyed the sight of the naked boy on his hands and knees wiping up the cum. He watched the boy's tight little ass wiggling as he mopped up the teenage juices. Coach felt his cock twitch inside his shorts. Felt it growing with new lust for this kid. But there would be time for that. They had the whole school year ahead of them.

The End

Here is a sample from another story you may enjoy:

DICK PARKER

COLIN AND DAVID

HOT GAY ROMANCE EROTICA

I was two weeks away from my twenty-third birthday and I lived with my parents and had no job. I was one of hundreds of thousands of "millennials" who had graduated from college and been unable to find a job in their field of study. Right now I'd take anything so I could get out of my parents' home and live on my own.

It's not that my parents aren't great. They are. But it's kind of sad living in the room I lived in when I was a teenager. It's not that I wasn't trying. I applied at every place that I could.

I did have a pretty good car thanks to Aunt Mary. She was my mother's only sister and she and I have been very close for years. Her husband died when I was a freshman in college and he left her well off. She lives on Lake Wisconsin on a huge place with nearly two acres of lakefront land. Her house could take care of a huge family but it was always just Aunt Mary, and her golden retriever, John. Yes, John, don't ask me how she came up with that name. I asked her once and she said he looked like a John.

Her lawn and garden were like something out of House and Garden magazine. When her husband died she put all of her energy into her home and garden. She asked me if I'd like to work for her to earn money during college and I jumped at the idea. I loved working outdoors and this was a great place to be. If I got too hot I could run out to the dock, jump into the lake, and take a swim. Aunt Mary paid me well and took care of me with great food and lots of extras.

She only had one daughter who ran off when she was seventeen and was never heard from again, so I was her favorite.

I heard mom drive up and walk to the kitchen. She came in from the garage and her eyes were all red.

"Mom? What's wrong?

"David, Aunt Mary died this morning."

My heart dropped. I stood there unable to speak.

Mom came to me and hugged me and we both wept. I couldn't believe it. Aunt Mary was as lively and vivacious as anyone I'd ever known. I thought she'd live to be a hundred.

"How, mom?"

"It was a heart attack. She was at the nursery buying plants. I suppose they were something you were going to plant soon."

"We were starting a new rose garden," I said, my voice breaking.

"They said it was very quick. She just slumped over and she was gone."

I turned and walked to my room. I lay face down on my bed and cried until I fell asleep.

I woke an hour later and got up. Mom was in the kitchen.

"Mom, what about John?"

"He wasn't with her. He's probably at her house."

"I better go and take care of him. I have a key."

"Will you bring him here?"

"I don't know. He's getting old. Maybe I'll just say there with him. I don't want to upset his life if I don't have to. I'll call you from Aunt Mary's."

I drove to the lake and followed the county road that ran past her house. I hadn't been there for a couple of weeks because the planting season was just starting so we had planned on working on the coming weekend. Now she was gone and I'd never get to garden with her again. I felt my eyes fill with tears as I drove along.

I pulled into her driveway and shut off my car. I could hear John barking in the house. I opened the front door and the big lug bounded out and began jumping all over me. He was happy to see me.

"Go make a pee," I said.

John ran off across the lawn toward the water. I watched him and then I noticed a kid on the dock next door. He was sitting on the end of their dock. He was wearing a pair of cutoff jeans and nothing else. He had a fishing pole lying next to him and there was a bobber floating on the water.

He turned and looked when I walked down by the water and called John.

"Hello," I said.

"Aye," he responded.

If you enjoyed this sample then look for **Colin and David.**

Also by this Author:

<u>Blind Attractions</u>

<u>Hard Tune</u>

From the Author

Check my page on Amazon for Updates and interesting info.

Author Central - http://www.amazon.com/Keith-Yates/e/B005X917G4

If you enjoyed any of my books then please share the love and click like on my books in Amazon.

If you write me a review and send me an email I will send you a free book, or many.
(Just know that these emails are filtered by my publisher.)

Good news is always welcome.

One Last Thing, For Kindle Readers...

When you turn the page, Kindle will give you the opportunity to rate this book and share your thoughts on Facebook and Twitter. If you enjoyed my writings, would you please take a few seconds to let your friends know about it? Because... when they enjoy they will be grateful to you and so will I.

Thank You!

Keith Yates
keith_yates@awesomeauthors.org

www.ingramcontent.com/pod-product-compliance
Lightning Source LLC
Chambersburg PA
CBHW071350130626
46556CB00005B/2116